W9-CCS-883

Iowa Hawkeye Football Trivia For Kids

With a few fun facts about Iowa too!

How much do you know about
Iowa Hawkeye Football history,
Iowa City and the
University of Iowa?

You're never too young to learn about the
Black and Gold.

Written by: Amy Bucknell
Illustrated by: Linda Reuter

Acknowledgements

Thanks to my Mom for both giving me the idea to write this book and for illustrating it!

Thanks to my family for supporting this adventure. Especially my husband and two sons who may think I'm a little too crazy about the Hawks!

Thanks to all Iowa Hawkeye historians. Passing down your work to the next generation will help keep Iowa Hawkeye traditions alive.

Thanks to the University of Iowa. Your help with this project was greatly appreciated!

Thanks to Coach Hayden Fry. After giving this book your approval, I couldn't stop talking about it for days! That alone has made this book worth all of the effort.

Thanks to all Iowa Hawkeye Football players and coaches. You have made it fun to be a fan of Iowa Hawkeye Football.

Thanks to all great Hawkeye fans out there. Your favorite place is Kinnick Stadium, but you'll go anywhere to support the Hawks!

Forward

This book was written for children of all ages.
Each question asked will have two possible answers.
Young children can simply point to the picture representing the correct answer.
Older children can have the correct explanations read to them.
Each answer can get more in depth as your child grows.
Eventually, your little Hawk will be up to speed with the basic Iowa and Iowa Hawkeye Football trivia!

Copyright © 2006 by Amy Bucknell. 33270-BUCK
Library of Congress Control Number: 2006904221
ISBN: Softcover 1-4257-1577-X
      Hardcover 1-4257-1576-1

Licensed by the University of Iowa.

To order additional copies of this book, contact:
Xlibris Corporation
1-888-795-4274
www.Xlibris.com
Orders@Xlibris.com

Question #1
The state capital of Iowa was originally...

Des Moines

OR

Iowa City

The state capital of Iowa was originally Iowa City.

Iowa became a state December 28, 1846.
Fifty-nine days after becoming a state, Iowa's first university was founded. That university was the University of Iowa. At that time it was known as SUI (State University of Iowa). State was dropped from its name in 1964.

The Old Capitol Building, in the heart of the University of Iowa's campus, was used as the capitol only until 1857. It was then that Des Moines took over as Iowa's state capital. Des Moines was thought to be a better location for the capital since it is closer to the center of the state.

In 2001 there was a major fire inside of the Old Capitol Building. It has since been put through extensive restoration.

Important to note:

When Iowa City served as the capital of Iowa, football had not yet begun at the university. Football started at SUI in 1889.

Question #2
The state bird of Iowa is...

Herky the Hawk
OR

The Eastern Goldfinch

The state bird of Iowa is the Eastern Goldfinch.

The male Eastern Goldfinch has a bright yellow body with black on its wings, tail and head. It lives throughout Iowa and even stays in the winter.

Herky, the University of Iowa mascot, has very similar coloring to the Eastern Goldfinch. Obviously Herky is much larger and is associated with the University of Iowa.

Important to note:

Herky has been the mascot at University of Iowa athletic events since the 1950's. In the last fifty-plus years, he has undergone small changes to update his appearance. One change apparent to young football fans is that Herky now wears a football helmet to Hawkeye Football games.

Herky attends more than just football games, however. In the mid 1990's, it was determined that Herky made around four hundred public appearances each year.

It is hard to believe that Herky hasn't been the only mascot at the University of Iowa. During the 1908 and 1909 football seasons, Iowa had a live bear cub named "Burch" as their mascot. He did not stand the test of time.

Unlike Burch, Herky is around to stay. He is well-known and loved by all Hawkeye fans…young and old!

Question #3
The Iowa Hawkeye football team currently plays football at...

Iowa Field

OR

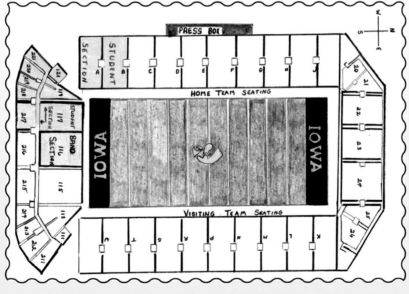

Kinnick Stadium

The Iowa Hawkeye football team currently plays football at Kinnick Stadium.

The first football field for the university was located east of the Iowa River and named Iowa Field. This field was used until 1929 when Iowa Stadium was completed west of the Iowa River. This new stadium was renamed Kinnick Stadium in 1972. The name Kinnick originated with the Hawkeye's first Heisman Trophy winner, Nile Kinnick.

Important to note:

When Iowa Stadium was first built in 1929, the seating capacity for the stadium was close to 53,000 fans.

In 1956, seats added to the south end zone increased capacity to 60,000.

In 1983, the north end zone was enclosed to increase capacity to 66,000.

After the 2006 renovations (including indoor suites, club seating, new south end zone and wider seats), Kinnick Stadium will hold around 70,000 fans.

The average attendance at Iowa Stadium during the 1939 season (Nile Kinnick's Heisman Trophy season) was 32,375.

The school record for highest average attendance in Kinnick Stadium was set in 2004 with an average of 70,397.

Question #4
Which Iowa Hawkeye Football helmet resembles one worn by an Iowa Football player in the 1960's?

I Helmet

OR

Tiger Hawk Helmet

The I Helmet

The tiger hawk became a symbol for the Hawkeyes in the late 1970's when Coach Hayden Fry took over the football program. Hayden thought the whole program was ready for a new look. The appearance of the uniforms with the new tiger hawk was just one example of the changes that Hayden had in store for the Hawkeyes. The tiger hawk was put on the helmet at that time, and it has remained there (with few exceptions) since.

There must be something appealing about the tiger hawk as its popularity has remained high. It has been associated with the University now for over 25 years and continues to be used on all types of Hawkeye products.

Important to note:

The University has used more than one design of the tiger hawk. The original design, however, still remains the most popular.

Question #5
A member of the "Ironmen" may have worn which helmet and jersey?

OR

The long sleeve jersey and old-fashioned helmet were worn by the football players known as the "Ironmen."

In the late 1930's, there was a group of football players for Iowa that were given the name "Ironmen." These players earned that name because they played both offense and defense. This meant the Ironmen played a majority of the game without a break. This is unlike today's college football players, where many play only offense, defense or special teams.

The way the game is played hasn't been the only change over the years. Notice, the older helmet didn't have much for padding or a facemask. The jersey did not have large shoulder pads underneath it either. The football players today have the advantage of much safer football equipment.

Important to note:

Nile Kinnick, Heisman Trophy winner of the 1939 Ironmen, played every minute for six games in a row his final year at Iowa. That is unheard of for today's college football player.

Question #6
"The Swarm" is...

the Iowa Football players swarming to tackle an opponent

OR

the Iowa Football players coming on and going off the playing field as a team

"The Swarm" is the Iowa Football players Coming on and going off the playing field as a team.

The swarm began during the Hayden Fry Coaching era. Hayden started this tradition because he felt it brought the team a sense of togetherness and family. He also felt that the sea of black jerseys Coming onto the field together would have an effect on the opposing team.

Coach Fry used his psychology background to start many new traditions at the University of Iowa. Like the tiger hawk that Hayden helped become a Hawkeye symbol, the swarm remains a strong Iowa Football tradition.

Important to note:

Hayden Fry also had the visiting locker room in Kinnick Stadium painted pink as a psychological tactic. He hoped it would have a calming effect on the visiting team and, if nothing else, distract his opponents. When the renovations of Kinnick Stadium took place in 2005, the new visiting locker room was designed in shades of pink to keep Hayden's tradition intact.

Question #7
When the announcer in Kinnick Stadium
asks if you are ready for
"The Boom," he is referring to...

the game opening kick-off
OR

the start of the Hawkeye Marching
Band pre-game performance

"The Boom" refers to the start of the Hawkeye Marching Band pre-game performance.

The marching band at the University of Iowa has 240 members. They are all students at the university, but not all are band or music majors. Any student attending the University of Iowa can participate in the band if he or she can pass the audition.

The band plays at all home games, at least one road game, and a bowl game when the Hawks qualify.

Important to note:

The marching band would not be complete without Iowa's Golden Girl. The Golden Girl is the baton twirler with the Hawkeye Marching Band. While other universities choose to have many baton twirlers, Iowa chooses to feature only one. This individual is usually a very distinguished twirler and receives a full ride scholarship through the athletic department.

If you have ever seen old Iowa Football film, you may have noticed the Scottish Highlanders. The Scottish Highlanders first performed at Iowa Football games in 1937. They started as an all male bagpipe band, admitted women during World War II and then became co-ed in 1972. The Scottish Highlanders last played at Iowa Football games in the early 1980s.

The spirit squads for the Iowa Hawkeyes also provide excitement and organize cheers for 70,000 Hawkeye fans. With their help, the fans assure that Kinnick Stadium is one of their opponents' toughest places to play.

Question #8
Floyd of Rosedale is...

a bull

OR

a pig

Floyd of Rosedale is a pig.

Floyd is now a trophy that resides with the winner of the Minnesota-Iowa game each year. Floyd was first involved in the game in 1935. That year, the governors of both states bet a pig on the outcome of the game. Unfortunately, Iowa lost this battle and had to give Minnesota a live full-blooded pig, Floyd of Rosedale. Since then, the winning school has received a trophy modeled after Floyd instead of the real pig! As of 2005, Minnesota leads Iowa in the series for Floyd 38-30-2.

The trophy with the bull is called the Heartland Trophy. This trophy stays with the winner of the Wisconsin-Iowa game for the year. The first year competing for this trophy was in 2004. The Hawks not only won this first showdown for the bull, but they also tied up the series between Iowa and Wisconsin (which was 39-39-2 as of 2005).

Important to note:

The Hawks also play Iowa State for the Cy-Hawk Trophy. As of 2005, Iowa holds a 35-18 advantage in the series dating back to 1894.

Which of these two ideas drove the 2002 Hawkeyes to victory?

"Break the Rock"

OR

"Pass the Pigskin"

"Break the Rock" motivated the Iowa Hawkeyes to success in the 2002 football season.

The idea behind "breaking the rock" is that success, or reaching a goal, is achieved not only in the final moment. It is achieved most commonly during all the hours spent preparing for the moment. The practice, the weight-lifting, and all the preparation that leads up to Saturdays often goes unnoticed. Without these things, however, there may be little success. "Break the Rock" can help remind us that our goal is only the final snapshot of all that has been put into it.

In 2002, the Hawks ended up Co-Champions of the Conference. In 2004, they achieved that honor again. It was in 2004 the Hawks depended more on their passing game, as many injuries plagued the Hawkeye backfield. Although it wasn't officially the motto in 2004, "pass the pigskin" was on the minds of many Hawkeyes late in that season.

Important to note:

There is more to Iowa Football than just Kinnick Stadium. The facilities for the football players at Iowa are outstanding. There are the Kenyon Practice Complex containing three outdoor practice fields (two natural and one artificial turf), "The Bubble" (indoor practice field), and the Jacobsen Athletic Building (houses the largest weight room in the conference as of 2005), among other facilities.

Question #10

When they are not playing or practicing football, the Iowa Hawkeye football players...

have to attend classes at the University of Iowa

OR

don't have to take classes like other students

Iowa Hawkeye football players, like all college athletes, are student-athletes.

They are in college to receive an education. The education must come first because if players do not go to class and maintain good grades, they become ineligible to play football. The majority of college football players, including those at the University of Iowa, do not go on to play professional football. Therefore, it is important for each football player to do well in school not only to stay eligible, but also to earn a degree.

Those Hawkeyes who are very successful on the field have found careers in football. As of 2005, there were at least thirty different Hawkeyes playing professional football for at least twenty different teams.

Important to note:

The Gerdin Athletic Learning Center, an academic center for all student-athletes at the University of Iowa, was built in 2003. This facility and its staff can help keep student-athletes on the right educational path.

Question #11
Which of these is Mount Rushmore?

OR

Mount Rushmore, a national memorial located in South Dakota, is the top picture.

Mount Rushmore is a monument of four former presidents of the United States (Washington, Jefferson, Roosevelt, and Lincoln). Each of these Presidents made a big impact on our nation's history. Although the lower picture is not a true monument, one could make a case that those four individuals have had a big impact on Iowa Hawkeye Football history.

The four pictured are:

Kirk Ferentz : 42-31 in six seasons at Iowa as head coach
8th place national finish three straight years
Two conference titles in the first six seasons

Hayden Fry : 143-89-6 in twenty seasons at Iowa
Three conference titles
College Football Hall of Fame Coach

Forest Evashevski : 52-27-4 in nine seasons at Iowa
Two conference titles
1958 national championship
College Football Hall of Fame Coach

Nile Kinnick : Winner of Heisman, Walter Camp, and Maxwell Trophies 1939

(This is a very limited list of their accomplishments)

The truth is that there are many Hawkeyes that have made a big impact on Iowa Football. Iowa may not have a monument like the one in South Dakota, but they do have the Athletics Hall of Fame Building. If you want to find out more about Hawkeye Football legends, and also many other sports at the University, the Athletic Hall of Fame Building is just the place to visit.

Until then, I hope you have learned more about the Hawkeyes. See you on Saturday in Kinnick. Go Hawks!